Bad Luck Charm

I was lying on my stomach, carefully scraping away at the side of square 8, when my trowel suddenly clicked against something hard.

"Only a rock," I said to Kate, ready to dump it.

"Wait a second." Kate took a good look at the gray rock through her glasses. "Aren't those markings?"

She helped me pick more dirt away from it, a speck at a time.

"Kate," I said softly, "doesn't it look like . . ."

"A rabbit!" Kate said. "A little carved stone rabbit, like . . ."

"Like the charms in *Shaman's Revenge!*" I almost dropped it.

Look for these and other books
in the Sleepover Friends Series:

SLEEPOVER FRIENDS

Lauren's Treasure

Susan Saunders

AN
APPLE
PAPERBACK

SCHOLASTIC INC.
New York Toronto London Auckland Sydney

ISBN 0-590-41695-2

12 11 10 9 8 7 6 5 4 3 2 1   8 9/8 0 1 2 3/9

Printed in the U.S.A.   28

First Scholastic printing, October 1988

Chapter 1

Have you ever noticed how nobody's satisfied with her hair? Curly-haired girls like my friend Stephanie Green want to have straight hair, and girls with hair as straight as a stick like Patti Jenkins and me — I'm Lauren Hunter — are dying to have curls. Every issue of every teen magazine shows someone getting a makeover. "Problem: Samantha's face is long and thin — what kind of hairstyle will make it look fuller? Solution: First, she shouldn't part it at all. Second, Samantha should brush her hair away from her face and try for fullness on the sides — a perm might be in order." And in the last photograph, there's Samantha, looking fabulous. Of course, she's a model, so she looked pretty to begin with.

1

Well, *my* face is long and thin, and my hair parts itself in the middle whether I want it to or not. It's medium brown and fine, and it's always falling into my face instead of out of it. It hangs absolutely flat on the sides, too. In other words, my hair is a major disappointment, and I've tried everything: curling it, braiding it, moussing it, gelling it.

"A body wave would take care of things," Stephanie told me. She and Patti and Kate Beekman and I were having lunch in the Riverhurst Elementary School Cafeteria. Now that I think of it, Kate likes *her* hair, and why not? It's thick, and blonde, and never out of place.

Stephanie was poking a gray mound on her plate with her fork. "What is this stuff, anyway?"

Patti examined her own plate carefully. " 'Wafer steak on a bun,' " she quoted from the school menu. " 'Carrot rings, and chilled plums.' "

"Yuck! What are we eating tonight at your house?" Stephanie asked Kate. It was Kate's turn to have our Friday sleepover.

Kate and I have lived practically next door to each other on Pine Street in Riverhurst since we were born. We started playing together while we were in diapers, and we've been best friends since kindergarten, which is when the Friday-night sleepovers started. Back then, we'd dress up in our moms' clothes and play Grown-Ups, or Let's Pretend. Dr. Beekman, Kate's dad, named us the Sleepover Twins, and for years it was just the two of us.

In the fourth grade, Stephanie moved from the city to a house at the other end of Pine Street. She and I were both in Mr. Civello's class, and sometimes we hung around together after school. I liked Stephanie because she was fun: She knew all the latest dance steps and a lot about clothes, and she told terrific stories about living in the city.

Stephanie and Kate didn't get along at all at first. Kate thought Stephanie was a show-off and a scatterbrain, and Stephanie thought Kate was so sensible that she was stuffy.

My older brother Roger had an explanation for their complaints: "They're too much alike — both bossy!"

Let's just say that each of them had her own way of doing things, and those ways often went in different directions. Still, I asked Stephanie to one of our sleepovers, and she invited Kate and me to spend a night at her house. Little by little, Kate and Stephanie started getting used to each other.

Then Patti Jenkins turned up in 5B, our fifth-grade class, this year. Although Patti and Stephanie couldn't be less alike — Patti's quiet, shy, and serious — Stephanie wanted Patti to be part of our group. They're both from the city, and they actually knew each other in first grade. Since Kate and I liked Patti right away, it wasn't long before there were *four* Sleepover Friends.

Food is a major part of our sleepovers, along with Truth or Dare, late-night movies, and lots of talking, so Kate had already planned the menu for that night. "First we're having Chinese food — Dad's bringing home take-out," she told Stephanie. "Then there'll be the usual super-fudge" — Kate makes that herself, with lots of dark chocolate and marshmallow whip — "and barbecue potato chips with Lauren's special dip." The dip is my own creation, developed over the years: onion soup, olives, bacon-bits, and sour cream. "And Dr Pepper, of course, and there's also Mom's banana cake left over from a dinner party last night."

Stephanie pushed her plate away and looked relieved. "Why are we bothering with this mess at all?" she asked. "I'm dieting, anyway. So what about a perm, Lauren?"

4

"I can't afford a body wave at Cut-Ups," I said to Stephanie. Cut-Ups is a hair salon in the Riverhurst mall. "Just a haircut costs forty dollars."

"You wouldn't have to go to Cut-Ups, Lauren," Stephanie said. "I could give you a body wave."

"Just like that?" I said. "Since when do you know about giving perms?"

"Since I read *Beauty on Five Dollars a Day*. A body wave is like rolling your hair, only it takes a little longer. Want to try it tonight?" she suggested.

"I don't know. . . ." I was remembering some of Stephanie's earlier beauty projects, like the avocado face mask to tighten our pores that my dog Bullwinkle went crazy over — after we'd already smeared it on our faces.

"The worst that can happen is that the permanent won't take and you'll be back where you started," Stephanie said. "What have you got to lose?"

Kate grinned. "Her hair, maybe. That perm stuff is really strong."

Stephanie frowned at her. "Lauren is not going to lose her hair. We'll do it tonight, and you'll have a whole new look at Chesterfield tomorrow," Stephanie said to me.

"Oh . . . why not?" I agreed at last. All the kids at Chesterfield who'd never met me before would think of me as Lauren Hunter, the girl with the curly brown hair.

As you probably could guess from its name, our town, Riverhurst, is on the banks of a river. The river is the Pequontic. About five miles up the Pequontic from Riverhurst there's a huge estate named Chesterfield.

All the schools in the area take class trips to Chesterfield to visit the mansion and the garden, which have been kept just as they were in the old days.

A few months ago, some scientists started digging away part of the lawn near the river. They turned up coins and buttons and glass bottles from before the Civil War, pottery from around the time of the American Revolution, and even an Indian spearhead almost a thousand years old. They invited school kids to help them dig on weekends, and Kate, Patti, Stephanie, and I had signed up for the next two Saturdays.

"Give up our Saturdays to crawl around in the dirt?" Stephanie hadn't been thrilled at first. She's definitely not the outdoor type.

"I think it'd be kind of neat to see who was living

6

here hundreds of years ago," Kate said, and Patti and I agreed with her.

"Besides, we'll meet lots of new kids," I told Stephanie. "I heard that fourth and fifth and sixth graders will be coming all the way from Dannerville and Hampton."

"I'll get my mom to pack lunches for us," Kate added slyly. Mrs. Beekman's an excellent cook, and Stephanie is her biggest fan.

Stephanie shrugged. "Well . . . I really wouldn't have anybody to do anything with if I stayed here and you guys went. . . ."

When she started planning the perfect outfit for digging, I knew she'd given in. "I've got a red checked sweatshirt, and I'll wear my black jeans." Stephanie's favorite color combination is red, black, and white. "What do you think — rubber boots, high-tops, or regular sneakers?" Kate, Patti, and I just smiled at one another.

That afternoon after school, as we walked over to the bike rack, Patti said, "I could buy the perm stuff for you at Romano's, Lauren. It'd probably be cheaper." Romano's is a discount store at the mall that sells just about everything.

Patti was going to the mall with her mother and

her little brother, Horace. Horace is six years old and super-intelligent. Actually, he's an okay kid, considering he collects lizards and turtles and other creepy-crawlies. Horace needed to buy some dried flies at Feathers and Fins for his pets, and Patti was returning a blouse her mom had bought her at Just Juniors.

"Thanks, Patti. That'd be great. I'll pay you back at Kate's tonight," I said.

"You're getting a home perm, Lauren?" Uh-oh. It was Jenny Carlin, eavesdropping.

Jenny's a girl in Mrs. Mead's room whom I don't like very much. She's had it in for me since the beginning of the year, because she liked Pete Stone, a boy in our class, and he started liking me. Actually, I don't like her at all, and she can't stand me. I'm not interested in Pete — he turned out to be totally immature — but Jenny won't let up.

Kate took one look at Jenny's smirk and snapped, "So what?"

"So nothing." Jenny glanced at me out of the corner of her eye. She's small, with tiny hands and feet, a button nose, and long hair. Since I'm the tallest girl in fifth grade next to Patti, Jenny makes me feel like a moose. "I'm glad Lauren's finally starting to take an interest in her looks, that's all." Like I was a total hag, or something! Then Jenny murmured to her sidekick, Angela Kemp, who was hanging on her every word. They both giggled.

"Oh — hi, Pete!" Stephanie called out suddenly and waved hard.

Jenny whirled around to look for Pete Stone, only to discover that Stephanie had been waving at a stop sign. "Ha, ha — fooled you!" Stephanie grinned.

Jenny scowled. She was just about to say something rude when her mother's car stopped at the curb. "See you tonight, Angela," she muttered instead.

Then, as the car pulled away, Jenny rolled down her window and called out, "Have fun playing beauty parlor, Lauren!"

I heard laughter behind me on the sidewalk, and with a sinking feeling in my stomach I turned to see half the boys from 5B walking past!

Chapter
2

That evening, Stephanie, Patti, Kate, and I grabbed a bunch of munchies from the Beekmans' kitchen and went straight upstairs to Kate's bedroom.

"Might as well get this over with," I said, feeling like the last scene in a prison movie.

I sat on the desk chair in front of the mirror, and Stephanie started rolling up my hair.

I was in charge of handing her the little papers you fold around the ends of each clump, and Patti was in charge of handing her the plastic curlers. Kate seemed to be in charge of handing her the food — after all, Stephanie hadn't eaten lunch, so she was making up for lost calories.

Kate picked up the TV listings for the evening

and reported, "Two great features on Friday Chillers: *Curse of the Undead* and *Shaman's Revenge*. This says *Shaman's Revenge* is about a guy who steals an Indian tribe's magic charms and dies a slow and gruesome death."

Kate'll watch any movie, not just once but four or five times. She'd like to be a movie director some day. Recently she's been especially interested in horror films, because she read somewhere that they're cheap to make and a good way to get started in the business.

"Sounds terrific," I said unenthusiastically. I don't really enjoy scary movies. Kate has always teased me about letting my imagination run away with me, and a Friday Chiller is just the sort of thing to make it fly completely out of control.

"Curler," Stephanie said to Patti after she'd swallowed a piece of fudge. "I wonder if there are any medicine men's charms lying around Chesterfield?"

"I read about the Indians who lived near Riverhurst in one of Dad's books," Patti told us. Both of Patti's parents are history professors at the university, so they have lots of old books.

"They were called the Yellow Paint People.

They were hunters and fishermen, so we're probably more likely to find arrowheads, spear points, and fishhooks than charms.''

"Why were they called Yellow Paint People?'' Kate asked her.

"Because whenever they buried a tribe member, they sprinkled yellow powder all over the grave,'' Patti answered. "It lasts for thousands of years without losing its color.''

"So if we dig up any yellow powder, we'd better watch out for bones,'' Kate said.

"You mean we might actually find human bones?'' Stephanie squealed, giving my hair an accidental yank. "Sorry, Lauren.''

Patti shrugged. "I guess it's possible,'' she said.

"Gross me out!'' said Stephanie. "Kate, would you mind scooping up some dip for me on a chip?'' Not gross enough to affect her appetite, I guess.

Kate handed Stephanie a chip piled with special dip. "You want some, Lauren?''

"No, thanks.'' Usually I have an enormous appetite, but I was starting to feel a little queasy. "Human bones?'' I repeated. Maybe this trip to Chesterfield wasn't such a hot idea.

"Don't start, Lauren.'' Kate had caught a glimpse

of my expression in the mirror. "If there *are* any bones, they'll be a thousand years old, and it won't matter to them *who* digs them up."

"Still . . ." I said. "It's kind of creepy. . . ."

"How many curlers have we got left?" Stephanie asked Patti.

"Um, seven," Patti answered.

"Hmmm." Stephanie combed through the unrolled hair that was hanging down around the bottom of my head and looked thoughtful.

"Aren't seven enough?" I asked her. We'd already used almost all the plastic curlers Stephanie and I had collected from our moms — about forty or fifty altogether.

"I guess so," Stephanie replied. "The instructions say to use fewer on the bottom, anyway."

She divided my hair into seven large chunks and rolled them around the curlers that were left.

"That does it." Stephanie stepped back to look at the results and gave my head a satisfied thump.

I peeked in the mirror. My head looked like something out of "I Love Lucy Meets Lost in Space."

"Now what?" Kate asked Stephanie.

"Now we go into the bathroom and squirt on the waving lotion," Stephanie said. "Come on, Lauren." She grabbed the pink bottle of lotion off Kate's desk.

The door to the bedroom was closed to keep out Melissa the Monster, Kate's little sister. Melissa's in the second grade, and it would be hard to say which she'd like better: crashing our sleepover or getting us into serious trouble.

When we pushed the door open, Fredericka, Kate's calico kitten, was sitting just outside it. Kate scooped her up, and we trooped down the hall to the bathroom. All of us crowded in and closed the door.

"We'll need a towel," Stephanie said.

Kate handed her one out of the cabinet, and Stephanie wrapped it around my shoulders. "Wipe off any lotion that gets on your skin," Stephanie warned me. "It could burn you."

Burn me? What would it do to my hair?

Stephanie opened the bottle, and started squirting pink liquid on each curler.

"Hey, what are you doing in here?" Melissa pushed the door open, but she retreated fast, making gagging noises. Fredericka raced out behind her.

"Mommy, they're making tear gas in the bathroom!" Melissa was yelling as she tore down the stairs.

I hated to agree with the kid, but the waving lotion was certainly making *my* eyes water!

"Melissa's been watching cop shows again," Kate said, but I noticed she was now holding *her* breath.

"How long do we have to leave this on?" I asked Stephanie, holding my nose.

"Twenty minutes, then the neutralizer in the white bottle for three minutes, and you're done." Stephanie coughed, and wheezed.

"Let's get out of this tiny bathroom before we suffocate!" Kate gasped, throwing the door open.

"So what should we do for twenty minutes?" I asked when we were back in Kate's room. "Not anything that requires any thought — the fumes are turning my brain to mush."

"Want to listen to requests on WBRM?" Patti suggested. "It's ten o'clock."

WBRM is a Riverhurst radio station, and they play requests for two hours on Friday nights.

"Sure." Kate switched her radio on.

There was a knock at the door and Mrs. Beek-

15

man peered into Kate's room. "What was Melissa talking about when she said 'tear gas'?" Mrs. Beekman asked. "Oh . . . I see." She'd gotten a whiff of the lotion.

"Not *see*. *Smell*, Mom." Kate giggled.

"Your dad's gone back to the hospital, Melissa's already in bed, and I'm about to be myself — I've got a splitting headache," Mrs. Beekman told Kate. "Try to keep the noise down to a dull roar, okay, girls?"

"Right, Mom," Kate said. "We will."

"And don't stay up too late. You've got a big day tomorrow. Your poor hair, Lauren," she added with a cautious sniff.

"It's going to look great, Mrs. Beekman," Stephanie said.

"I thought it looked fine just the way it was," Mrs. Beekman said before she shut the door. But mothers always say that.

"It's request time, guys and gals!" shouted the WBRM deejay. "This is Rockin' Ralphie, with a request from Tod S. to Mary Beth Y., with love: 'Won't You Please Forgive Me?' "

"They must be fighting again," Stephanie said.

16

Tod Schwartz is the quarterback on the River-hurst High School football team. He lives across the street from Stephanie. Mary Beth Young is his steady girlfriend, and they break up about twice a month.

"Doesn't Mary Beth kind of remind you of Jenny Carlin? They're both always giggling and shrieking and rolling their eyes when boys are within a mile of them," Kate said thoughtfully.

Just the mention of Jenny Carlin's name made me steam! "I'd sure like to send in a request to her!" I muttered. "Like 'You're So Vain'! Or even better, 'You're a Jerk,' by the Lurkers!"

"Why don't we?" said Stephanie.

"Why don't we what?" Kate asked.

"Phone in a request for Jenny!" Stephanie picked up a pencil and Kate's memo pad. "He usually gives the number at the end of every song."

"We're taking requests here!" Rockin' Ralphie announced. "Call five-five-five-four-eight-nine-five, and dedicate a song to the one you love . . . or hate! Heh, heh, heh."

"Five-five-five-four-eight-nine-five," Stephanie repeated as she wrote it down. She handed the paper to Kate.

The Beekmans' upstairs phone is in the hall. Kate started for the door, then turned to ask, "Who should we say it's from?"

It was Patti who came up with, "Well-meaning friends."

We burst out laughing. "Excellent!" said Kate.

She crept out into the hall, picked up the phone, and dialed the number. "Hello — WBRM requests?" she whispered as loudly as she dared with her mom only a few doors away. "I'd like to dedicate a song to Jenny C . . . from well-meaning friends. . . . Right . . . the song is 'You're a Jerk,' by the Lurkers . . . thanks very much." Very quietly she hung the phone up, and we darted back into her room.

Chapter
3

"I can't believe we did that!" Stephanie squealed after Kate had closed the door. All of us were giggling our heads off.

"I just hope Jenny Carlin hears it," I said. "What if she isn't listening?"

"Don't worry — if she's *not* listening, somebody else'll tell her about it," Kate replied. "Oh, the guy who answered the phone at WBRM said they were pretty stacked up with requests. They probably won't be playing ours for at least thirty minutes."

Stephanie looked at Kate's alarm clock. "That gives us plenty of time to finish Lauren's hair."

We tiptoed back into the bathroom so I could stick my head under the shower to wash off the waving lotion. Then Stephanie squirted the neutralizing liquid on my curlers. Three minutes later she started unrolling them.

"Well, it's definitely curly," Kate said.

The top of my head looked as if it were covered with bouncy little springs. I kind of liked it.

The bottom was a different story, though. The seven chunks of hair Stephanie had rolled up last barely curled at all. In fact, they mostly stuck out at seven different angles.

"What do you think about this?" I pointed to the stiff fringe of hair around the bottom.

"Oh, it'll be fine once it dries," Stephanie said quickly.

"It will," said Patti, nodding helpfully.

You can always count on Melissa to tell the truth, however — whether you want to hear it or not. She pushed open the bathroom door, whining, "Aren't you guys ever coming out?" When she caught sight of my hair, she snickered. "Lauren, you look like a Triceratops!"

"Melissa, get OUT OF HERE!" Kate thundered.

The Monster crossed her eyes at her sister and closed the door.

"Who's Triceratops?" I asked Kate.

20

"Oh, Melissa's class is studying dinosaurs," Kate mumbled. "Triceratops is the one with kind of a . . . a . . . ruffle around its neck."

"Thanks a lot, Stephanie," I said crossly, trying to bend down the hair sticking straight out around *my* neck. "I've really been wanting to look like a dinosaur."

"Don't be silly." Stephanie combed the hair down, but it sprang right back up.

"Well?" I said, frowning at her in the bathroom mirror.

"We'd better get back to the radio," warned Kate. "It must almost be time."

In Kate's room, we listened to the end of a song called, 'Always, Forever,' from Tug K. to Barbara B. Tug's another football player at Riverhurst High, and Barbara Baxter's a cheerleader.

Then the deejay announced, "And now, from some well-meaning friends to Jenny C., as in Cow . . ."

"Oh, no!" Kate moaned. "We didn't say *that*!"

"Jenny," Rockin' Ralphie went on, "if these are your *well-meaning friends*, you sure don't need any enemies." He cackled. " 'You're a Jerk,' by the Lurkers!"

21

"You're a *jerk*! How did you *get* that way? What a *jerk*!" the Lurkers screamed.

"C for Cow. That's awful," Patti said. Then she exploded into giggles.

"Would I love to see J-Jenny Carlin's f-face right now!" Stephanie was laughing so hard she was stuttering.

"One point in our favor," I said. Even if my hair was acting strange, *I* was feeling better. "Let's celebrate. Is there anything to eat downstairs?"

Kate clicked the radio off. "Let's go get the banana cake."

Stepping over the squeaky third step so we wouldn't wake Melissa, the four of us sneaked down to the kitchen.

The Beekmans have a huge refrigerator, and I've probably eaten at least a thousand pounds of food out of it over the years.

"What's in that dish?" I asked, peering into the fridge over Kate's shoulder.

Kate slid the dish out and took off the top. "Cold sweet potatoes. Want some?"

I took a few spoonfuls of sweet potatoes, a slice of roast pork, and some green beans. The Chinese take-out was great, but it didn't seem to stick with me.

"Lauren, you really depress me!" Stephanie moaned. "How can you eat so much and stay so thin?" She stood on tiptoe and sucked in her cheeks. "Maybe if I were three inches taller . . ."

"Maybe if you jogged with Roger and me," I suggested. My brother and I jog three miles three times a week.

"You know jogging makes me sweat, and sweating makes my hair frizz."

"Please don't talk about hair right now!" I said.

"Don't worry," Stephanie said. "With a little styling, it's going to look great." She started digging through the fridge, too. "Where's that banana cake, Kate?"

We piled a lot of leftovers on a tray, opened another king-sized bottle of Dr Pepper, and carried everything into the living room.

"Friday Chillers," Kate reminded us, turning the TV on low.

When the picture came into focus, we were looking at a cowboy sitting next to a campfire in the desert. His Jeep was parked nearby, and it was loaded

down with picks and shovels and old Indian stuff —
a mound of broken pottery, a bag full of silver and
turquoise necklaces, even a pair of torn moccasins.

The cowboy really seemed excited about four
little carved stone animals he was holding in his
hand — he was sort of gloating over them and chuck-
ling to himself.

"The tribe's charms," Kate said.

"I think this guy's about to be in serious trouble,"
Stephanie mumbled around a mouthful of banana
cake.

An enormous gray cloud was rising up in the
dark sky. It looked just like an Indian with feathers
in his hair. The cloud Indian waved a long arm in
the cowboy's direction before it disappeared. Sec-
onds later, one of the little stone animals crumbled
to dust in the man's hand. And early the next morning, he got bitten by a diamondback rattlesnake!

Things went from bad to worse. The cowboy
could have died from the snakebite, all alone in the
desert, but he got over it after days of agony. Then
his Jeep broke down, and he was in danger of dying
of thirst. He'd collapsed on a sand dune, gasping and
choking. He pulled the three remaining stones out
of his pocket . . . and another one was turning to

dust before his swollen eyes . . . when the Beekmans' telephone rang.

"Grab it!" Kate hissed, and we all raced for the wall phone in the kitchen. Patti was fastest, so she picked it up.

"Hello?" She listened for a second, then said, "Yes, she is. Please hold on." Patti covered the mouthpiece of the phone with her hand. "Lauren, it's for you. It's a boy!" she murmured.

"You're kidding!" Mrs. Beekman was going to kill me for getting a phone call so late! "Who?" I whispered back.

"He didn't say."

Could it be Pete Stone? Or maybe Donald Foster? Donald lives in the house between Kate's house and mine. He's in the seventh grade, and he's just about the most conceited boy in Riverhurst. He could have been calling as a joke.

I cleared my throat and took the phone. "Hello?"

"Hello, Lauren?" It wasn't a voice I recognized, it was kind of gruff and crackly at the same time.

"Who is this?" I said.

"Oh, you don't know me. I'm from Dannerville. But I've seen you around," the voice said.

25

"Where?"

"Uh . . . the mall. I'm a friend of . . . uh . . . Pete Stone's. My name is Bradley. Bradley Michaels. I just thought I'd say hi."

"Hi, Bradley."

"Bradley?" Kate and Stephanie were mouthing at me. They didn't know anyone named Bradley, either. I shrugged.

"How did you know I was here?" I asked him.

"Uh . . . Pete told me you have . . . uh . . . sleepovers every Friday . . . I was calling to find out what you're doing tomorrow." Bradley's voice was strange — it went up and down as he talked. "I thought maybe we could meet at the mall . . . have some pizza . . . maybe even go to a movie."

I couldn't believe it! A boy was actually asking me out? Or at least to meet him. "I can't tomorrow," I had to tell him. "I'm going to Chesterfield with a bunch of kids from Riverhurst Elementary."

"What about Sunday afternoon? We could meet in front of Pizza Palace at two, or something."

"Well . . . maybe. How would I know you?" I asked him.

There was a long pause. "I'm tall . . ." Bradley's

voice cracked, and he cleared his throat. "I have blond hair, and blue eyes. . . ."

I thought I heard somebody giggle in the background. "What was that?" I asked, beginning to feel something wasn't quite right.

"Uh . . . it's . . ." Then Bradley started to giggle himself!

There was a lot of whispering, and then a new voice squealed into the phone, "Now who's the *jerk*, Lauren?"

It was Jenny Carlin, and *Bradley* was her sidekick, Angela!

Chapter
4

"They're incredible! They were going to get me to go to the mall to meet . . . this . . . *Bradley*," I sputtered after I'd slammed down the phone. "And he'd never show up, so I'd look like a total dork in front of Jenny Carlin and Angela Kemp!" I was *steaming*!

"Don't get yourself crazy, Lauren. You were on to them right away," Patti said soothingly.

"Why don't we play Mad Libs, or Truth or Dare?" Stephanie suggested, to change the subject.

"I think I've already played Truth or Dare tonight," I said gimly. "Only it was Jenny's game!"

Kate and Patti and Stephanie and I ended up going to bed. I took a last look in the mirror before

I climbed into Kate's dad's old sleeping bag. My hair was dry by then, but the top was still springy, and the bottom was still stiff.

"It'll look fine after you've slept on it," Stephanie said drowsily from her side of the double bed.

But when I woke up the next morning, I knew the only thing I could do to improve my hair was cover it up.

"With what?" Kate asked. I have a pretty big head.

"A lampshade, if necessary," I muttered huffily.

Mrs. Beekman made breakfast early, so we could all go home and get ready for the trip to Chesterfield. My parents were sitting in the kitchen, reading the newspaper, when I got to our house.

"Hi, sweetie." My mom barely glanced up before looking down at her paper again. Then she blinked hard, and her eyes focused on my head. "Lauren . . ." she said. "Your hair . . . I thought you said Stephanie knew what she was doing!"

"I know!" I wailed. "All I can hope is, the perm won't last long."

"I think it's kind of cute," said my father.

"Cute if you like dinosaurs!" I muttered. "I'm going upstairs to wash it — five or six times!"

The curls on top loosened up a little after I'd shampooed my hair till my scalp hurt, but the fringe around the bottom was still sticking out in different directions. I managed to jam most of it into one of Roger's high-school baseball caps before I got into the car.

Kate was carrying a big paper bag and a Thermos when Dad and I picked her up at nine-thirty. Mrs. Beekman had packed enough lunch for us all, as Kate had promised. She makes great tuna salad sandwiches with apple slices in them and a fruit salad with tiny marshmallows, called ambrosia, that's fabulous.

My dad drove to Stephanie's next. I got out of the car and rang the Greens' doorbell.

"Come in!" Stephanie called from inside the house. "I'm putting on my hiking boots." Then she yelled, "No — wait!"

But she was too late. I was already opening the front door. A fuzzy black cannonball shot past my ankles while Stephanie shrieked, "Cinders — you come back here!"

Cinders is Stephanie's kitten, a brother to Kate's kitten Fredericka, and Patti's Adelaide, and my

Rocky. Cinders is solid black, to go with Stephanie's red, black, and white color scheme.

"Grab him!" shouted Stephanie.

Cinders dashed around the side of the house, and Stephanie and I tore after him.

"Cinders has a new hobby!" Stephanie puffed as we followed the kitten into the Greens' backyard.

"What's that?" I said over my shoulder. My legs are about twice as long as Stephanie's, so I was leading even though I had to hang onto my cap while I ran.

"Driving the neighbors' dog bananas!" Stephanie replied.

I dived for Cinders's tail, but he scooted through some bushes and scrambled onto the top rail of the Greens' tall stockade fence.

"Did somebody finally move in behind you?" I asked. The house behind Stephanie's had been empty for months.

"Yeah, a couple of weeks ago. Hear that?" Stephanie said.

A long mournful howl floated over the fence, growing louder and more piercing.

"Their dog," Stephanie explained. "Watch Cinders — isn't he too much?" she giggled.

From the safety of the top rail, the black kitten peered down at the other side of the fence. Then he arched his back and hissed like a Halloween cat!

There was a tremendous thud as the dog in the neighbors' yard hurled himself at the fence, yapping and growling.

"The dog's too short," Stephanie said, "and Cinders knows it. Look at him."

Cinders was parading back and forth on the top rail with his tail stuck straight up in the air. His pointy white teeth were showing in what looked like a feline grin.

"Okay, that's enough," Stephanie said to Cinders as the dog thudded against the other side of the fence again. "You wouldn't be acting nearly so tough if there wasn't a solid fence between you and that poor animal." She pushed through the bushes and stood on tiptoe to pull Cinders off the top rail. "You're going to make us late, you bad cat!"

Stephanie carried Cinders back around the house and dumped him in the front hall. "We're going, Mom!" she called out.

"Have fun, girls." Mrs. Green handed Stephanie

a plastic bag of chocolate-chip cookies. "Fuel for digging. See you later."

Patti's house was the last stop, and then Dad dropped us off at Riverhurst Elementary. One of the school buses was parked out front with a noisy crowd around it. Mr. Civello was checking names off a list as each kid got on the bus. He and Mr. Miller, the assistant principal, would be in charge of the Riverhurst kids at Chesterfield.

There were some empty seats in the back, behind a skinny little boy with reddish hair, ears that stuck out, and brown glasses.

"Hey, Walter," Stephanie said as we walked past him.

"Hi, Stephanie!" He gave all four of us a big grin, turning around to see where we'd be sitting.

"Who is that?" I whispered. I'd certainly never seen him before.

"Yeah, do you have a secret life?" Kate teased Stephanie. "And what's he doing here? He looks like he's Melissa's age."

"His name is Walter Williams," Stephanie murmured. "It's his family that moved into the house behind ours. He probably isn't much older than Melissa, but he's a genius — his mother told mine Walter has an IQ of 175, or 190, or something — so he's in the fourth grade instead of second or third, where he should be."

"Why's he staring at me?" I said. "Is he weird, or am I looking worse than I thought?" I pulled Roger's cap further down on my head.

"Don't be so paranoid, Lauren," Kate scolded. "He probably likes your Riverhurst Raiders hat."

I took my sunglasses out of my backpack and slipped them on.

"Hey, Lauren, are you in some kind of disguise?" Kyle Hubbard — he's a kid in 5A — yelled from the front of the bus. He raced down the aisle toward us. "I'm glad to see you guys. I thought it was going to be all sixth-graders." He glanced at Walter Williams. "Or babies."

"You gave up a Saturday to do school stuff?" Kate asked as Kyle dropped into a seat across the aisle.

"I couldn't pass up a chance to find some moldy old bones, like in" — Kyle made a horrible face, stretched out his arms, and curved his fingers into claws — "*The Mummy's Tomb!*" he rasped, waving his claws at us. "Besides," Kyle admitted, "Mrs. Milton told me it might bring up my grade in social studies."

I noticed Walter Williams was frowning at him.

Kyle is stocky, with brown curly hair and big brown eyes. Actually, he's sort of cute. He and Kate got to be friends last year when they were in the same fourth-grade class. Kyle's a movie freak, too, but scary movies have always been his favorites. He can repeat long scenes from *The Mummy's Tomb* and *I Talked to a Zombie* word for word, he's seen them so many times.

Stephanie jabbed me with her elbow. "Pete Stone!" she whispered. "I'm surprised Jenny's not here!"

I thought Pete might come sit with us, too, but he flopped down next to Ricky Delman, a sixth-grader.

" 'When the sun rose over the tomb of the pharaoh,' " Kyle was going on in a hollow voice, " 'it shone on a grisly sight. The bloody and battered remains of Captain James . . .' "

"Would you please shut up, Kyle?" I asked, but it was more an order than a request. I hate *The Mummy's Tomb*!

Kyle had to stop, anyway, because Mr. Civello

35

and Mr. Miller had climbed onto the bus. "Please quiet down and take your seats," Mr. Miller called out. "We're on our way, on a trip back in time!" Mr. Miller can definitely be corny.

The doors slammed shut, and the bus lurched forward with a grinding of gears. It's a short trip to Chesterfield. We barely had time to eat any of Mrs. Green's cookies. The school buses from Dannerville and Hampton Elementaries were already in the parking lot when our bus turned in, and there were kids running all over the place.

"Wow — check out that guy!" Stephanie was staring out the window at the kid in a red-flannel shirt. "He looks just like Kevin DeSpain."

Kevin DeSpain's the star on *Made for Each Other*. He has dark hair and big green eyes and is definitely a hunk.

"He does not," said Kate, slipping on her glasses for a second. Kate's nearsighted, but she hates to wear them. "Not unless Kevin's turned into a chimp."

Patti and I giggled — the kid did have kind of long arms.

"You just think he's cute because he's wearing red," I said to Stephanie.

"Let's get off this thing and take a closer look!" Stephanie led the way up the aisle and down the steps. She didn't get any farther than the side of the bus, however.

"Ho-o-ld it, Green!" Mr. Civello said before Stephanie could dash off. "Okay, kids, we're dividing into two groups. One group, headed by Mr. Miller, will dig before lunch, and clean after. The other group, headed by me, will do the opposite."

Since Kyle, Stephanie, Patti, Kate, and I were standing together, we all ended up in Mr. Civello's group. "You, too, Williams," Mr. Civello said to Walter. He added three sixth-graders and four more fourth-graders to his group. Mr. Miller was in charge of the rest of the Riverhurst kids, including Pete Stone.

At Chesterfield, there's a big three-story brick mansion overlooking the river, four greenhouses full of strange plants, a giant fish pond, and a carriage house with two carriages and a Model-T Ford parked inside it. We Riverhurst kids walked up the gravel path between the mansion and the carriage house to a terrace under some trees, where a scientist was waiting to talk to us.

"I'm Ms. Anderson," she said. "I'm an archaeologist."

"I never thought of scientists as being so cool," Stephanie murmured. "Great earrings!"

Ms. Anderson was wearing tiny gold fish skeletons in her pierced ears. She had on faded jeans, an old sweatshirt with "Dig It!" on the front, and a terrific silver and turquoise Indian belt.

"Archaeologists learn about the people of earlier times by studying their tools or weapons or pottery, even their campfires — whatever they've left behind." Ms. Anderson grinned. "Some people call us 'garbalogists.' "

"Here at Chesterfield, we began by exposing the foundation of a one-hundred-fifty-year-old dock on the Pequontic," she went on. "Then we started finding things two hundred, three hundred, and even a thousand years old."

Ms. Anderson showed us some of the coins and buttons they'd already dug up, along with a dark-green glass bottle from 1790 and an Indian fishhook made of wood.

"We're doing important work here," Ms. Anderson said, "uncovering the history of this region, and we're very glad to have your help. If you have any questions at all as you're cleaning or digging, or if you're unsure about something, please ask me immediately. We can't afford to make mistakes. These objects are precious.''

Then Ms. Anderson led us around the mansion and down the sloping lawn toward the river.

The lawn had been marked off with stakes and white strings into twenty large squares, each of them numbered. Some of the squares were still grass-covered and green, in some of the squares the grass had been peeled back, and in others there was a hole where the lawn used to be.

''The diggers will be working in these squares,'' Ms. Anderson told us. ''Very carefully, with small trowels and nail files and even dentists' picks, you'll be removing the dirt a little at a time and sifting it through a screen.

''When the diggers find something,'' Ms. Anderson continued, ''it will go to the cleaners.'' She pointed to a group of long tables under the trees at the edge of the lawn. ''The cleaners will wash things with soft toothbrushes and water.

''Keeping records is important,'' Ms. Anderson said. ''If a digger finds a button, for example, he or she must write down the number of the square where the button was found, what part of the square, and exactly what the button looks like. The cleaners will use the lists to label things once they've been washed."

"Whew! This sounds like an awful lot of work!" Kyle muttered.

"If I'd known we were going to be up to our elbows in dishwater, I'd have packed some rubber gloves," Stephanie whispered. "My hands'll shrivel like prunes!"

"All clear so far?" Ms. Anderson was asking. "Please follow me."

Chapter
5

Since the Sleepover Friends were in Mr. Civello's group, we spent the morning being cleaners. Each table had room for eight people. In front of each place was a plastic washtub of water, a soft toothbrush, a small tray piled with muddy bits and pieces that had been dug up, and a handwritten list.

The four of us sat together, Kate at one end, and Patti, Stephanie, and I on a bench at one side of the table. Walter Williams slid down the bench across from from us until he was sitting directly in front of me. He gave me a big grin.

Stephanie was stirring through her tray of bits. "Think there's anything really gross here?" she murmured. Then she clutched my arm. "Lauren! Could this be . . . an evil charm!" She poked at a mud-covered blob.

"Very funny," I said, giving her a shove. Stephanie and Kate aren't afraid of anything, so I knew she was teasing. Besides, anybody could see it was broken pottery. "How many evil charms have you heard of with little blue flowers painted on them?"

"You've got sharp eyes." Ms. Anderson reached over Stephanie's shoulder to pick up the pottery. "Early 1800s, probably part of a bowl. It should clean up nicely."

She dipped it into Stephanie's washtub. "First dip it in water" — Ms. Anderson swished the piece of pottery around — "then brush it thoroughly with the toothbrush. See how all the caked dirt flakes off?"

Ms. Anderson put the piece of pottery back on Stephanie's tray. "You'll label it with the number it was given on the list, and the number of the square, and check it off. Then you'll go on to the next item. All set?"

"Yes, Ms. Anderson," Stephanie said.

I'd cleaned and labeled two buttons, a piece of broken pottery, and an iron hook — Ms. Anderson said it had been used to hang pots over a fire — when I felt someone watching me.

Walter Williams was so short that his chin barely came above the edge of the table. Still, he was peering right at me through his round brown glasses.

"Hey!" he said, smiling like the Cheshire Cat in Alice in Wonderland.

"Hey," I replied. The kid was definitely odd.

"I'm Walter Williams," he announced then. "But my friends all call me Walt." He sat up straight, waiting for me to say something.

"I'm Lauren Hunter," I said.

"You're a good friend of Stephanie's, aren't you? I think I've seen you together once or twice." Walter's big ears turned bright red.

This is how geniuses talk? I was thinking, when Kate nudged me with her sneaker.

"I think he *likes* you," she whispered in my ear. "Know what I mean?"

"Give me a break!" I hissed. "He's eight years old and three feet tall!"

But as the morning wore on, I started to think Kate might be right. When I dropped my toothbrush, who scrambled under the table for it? Walter! When Kyle teased me about the baseball cap — "You're using it to cover a bald spot, right, Lauren?" — who came to my rescue? Walter!

"You'd look good with a paper bag over your head!" he growled at Kyle.

"Whoa!" said Kyle. "New boyfriend, Lauren?"

It was too much! During our lunch break, Kate, Stephanie, Patti, and I carried our food down to the bank of the river.

"Maybe it'll give us some privacy," I said hopefully.

But who turned up, sitting on the next boulder? Walter!

"This is getting embarrassing," I whispered to the others.

"I think it's kind of sweet," Kate said and giggled. "He's dogging your tracks like a basset hound."

"Better you than me, Lauren," Stephanie said. "I'd have him hanging over my back fence all the time! Ick!"

After lunch, Patti, Kyle, and Walter Williams were assigned to square 10, and Kate, Stephanie, and I to square 8. The sides of our square looked like pieces of a layer cake. At the top there were plant roots, then a few inches of dark, sandy soil. Under that was a foot or two of hard, reddish clay, getting harder and redder as it got deeper. Toward the bottom of our square there were bunches of cream-colored pebbles, and some larger rocks, too.

When you're digging, you lie on your stomach outside the hole and use trowels and nail files to pick the dirt away from the sides and the bottom. If you find something, you put it in a tray at the edge of the hole, then write it up on a list. After you've picked away a little mound of dirt, you sift it through a screen to see if you've missed anything tiny.

Digging is a thousand times more fun than cleaning. It's kind of like a treasure hunt: you don't really know if you'll find anything at all, but you always have the *feeling* you're just about to turn up something absolutely fantastic!

Kate put on her glasses, squinted down into the hole at square 8, and spotted something right away.

"Look — next to this pebble. . . ." She used the end of her trowel to flip a pebble out of the clay layer. With a nail file, she slowly pried loose a small, shiny sliver that had been wedged in beside the rock.

"Blue glass," Kate said, laying the sliver in the tray.

"With lighter-colored blue bubbles," added Stephanie, peering closely at it.

Kate printed on the list under number 1: Square 8, middle of clay layer — small piece of blue glass with lighter-colored blue bubbles. Then she signed her name next to it.

"Wow — what's this?" Patti was exclaiming from square 10.

"It looks like an old lima bean to me," said Kyle.

But after Patti and Walter had brushed away the dirt, the lima bean turned out to be a green pottery bead with a hole running through the middle of it.

"Jewelry!" said Stephanie approvingly. "Maybe there are some gold rings lying around!"

Instead, she uncovered a hollow red tube about as long as one of her fingers. "I don't think this is anything," she said, ready to pitch it onto the mound of dirt outside the hole.

But Ms. Anderson walked over to take a look. "Always ask me before you get rid of something," she told us. "This happens to be a clay pipestem, and it's more than two hundred years old. Write it up on the list, please," she said to Stephanie.

After Ms. Anderson had checked out Patti's green bead, she added, "This was part of an Indian necklace or bracelet. Good work! Keep an eye peeled for more of these."

"If there are beads around here, can a pile of

moldering old bones be far behind?" Kyle said in his hollow voice, just in case we'd forgotten. He started digging like crazy.

The afternoon was getting pretty hot. "I think my fringe is wilting," I said to Kate and Stephanie, stuffing the bottom of my hair back under Roger's cap.

"I'm wilting myself," said Stephanie. "I'm going to the mansion for a drink." She stood up, dusted herself off, and headed across the lawn.

I was lying on my stomach, carefully scraping away at the side of square 8, when my trowel suddenly clicked against something hard. I grabbed a nail file and flicked the dirt away, until I'd uncovered what looked like a small, gray rock.

"Only a rock," I said to Kate, ready to pry it out and dump it.

"Wait a second." Kate took a good look at the gray rock through her glasses. "Aren't those markings?"

She helped me pick more dirt away from it, a speck at a time, until the rock fell out of the side of the hole and into my hand. It was small and rounded, with deep lines cut into it.

"Kate," I said softly, "doesn't it look like . . ."

"A rabbit!" Kate said. "A little carved stone rabbit, like . . ."

"Like the charms in *Shaman's Revenge*!" I almost dropped the rabbit. I halfway expected to see a cloud shaped like an Indian rising in a dark sky, waving a long arm at me. But the sun was as bright as ever.

"This could be important," said Kate. "We'd better tell Ms. Anderson."

"Let me write it down before I forget everything," I said. Next to the number 3 on the list, I printed, Square 8, bottom of clay layer — small, carved gray stone. . . .

I was just finishing printing "rabbit" when I heard Stephanie screech. "Hey, yellow paint! Kate! Patti! Lauren! It's the Yellow Paint People!"

I laid the gray stone rabbit in the tray, next to the blue glass and the pipestem. Kate and I scrambled to our feet and raced toward Stephanie at square 17, with Patti right behind us.

"Where are you going, Lauren?" Walter Williams shouted. I guess he'd been watching us dig out the rabbit.

I didn't bother to answer. It would only encourage him to keep talking, and I just wanted him to leave me alone.

Square 17 just happened to be the hole where the boy in the red-flannel shirt was digging. Ms. Anderson was already there, down on her hands and knees holding a small trowel, while Stephanie and the boy talked excitedly to each other.

"Wow!" said Patti, who was right behind us. "Just like it said in my dad's book!"

A yellow powder was starting to leak out of the bottom of the square hole. Every time Ms. Anderson touched it with her trowel, she uncovered more powder.

"Which means that somewhere down there . . . ," Kate began.

". . . maybe even right under our feet . . ." I shifted uncomfortably in my sneakers.

" . . . there's an Indian grave. I certainly hope so." Ms. Anderson gave a satisfied nod. "Sorry, kids," she said to the boy in the red shirt, and another boy wearing a blue Hampton High sweatshirt miles too big for him. "You'll have to move out of this square — the graduate students from the university archaeology department will be taking over."

Practically everyone crowded around to watch

the grad students dig. There were two of them, a really cute guy with a blond flat-top and a thin girl with long brown hair in a braid. Besides trowels and nail files and dental picks, they had some tiny brushes and two round rubber balls with holes in one end that they squeezed to blow dirt away from where they were working.

At first, all they dug out of the hole at square 17 was more yellow powder. It was kind of dull gold, really, and sort of greasy-looking. "The Indians ground up a mineral to make it," Ms. Anderson explained.

Then the girl's pick caught on something in a corner of the hole. "I think I've got it," she said to Ms. Anderson.

Slowly and carefully, the grad students brushed and blew the soil away, until they'd uncovered a couple of inches of something smooth and cream-colored.

"Just another dumb rock," mumbled the boy in the red shirt.

"No," Ms. Anderson said. "If I'm not mistaken, that's a portion of a human skull."

"You're kidding!" I thought Kyle Hubbard was going to throw himself into the hole. "Is the rest of it there, too — the arms and legs *and everything?*"

A chill ran down my spine. "Kyle, please!" I said. "Do you have to go into details?"

"How old is it?" asked the kid wearing the blue sweatshirt.

"We'll have to complete the excavation before I can tell you that. I hope to have the answers to all your questions next week," Ms. Anderson said. "Now I'm afraid it's time for you to get back on your buses. Diggers, please bring your trays and lists to the tables."

Kate and Stephanie and I hurried back to square 8. Stephanie gathered up the tools, and Kate picked up the list.

"You haven't finished writing down about the rabbit, Lauren," she reminded me.

"What rabbit?" Stephanie asked.

"This one." I held the tray out to show her . . . and that's when I realized the gray stone rabbit was missing!

The sliver of blue glass was still there, and Stephanie's clay pipestem. But the carved rabbit was gone!

"Kate, it's disappeared!" I looked around on the ground where the tray had been. I even glanced up at the sky, just in case. Had the rabbit crumbled to dust, the way the one in the movie had? "I hope there aren't any rattlesnakes around Riverhurst," I muttered. "Or I'm definitely a goner!"

"Try to think clearly," Kate said, taking the tray. "What about your pockets?"

I went through all my pockets. I found an old Life-Saver covered with fuzz in one of them, but nothing else. "Besides, I *know* I put the rabbit in the tray," I told Kate, "just before I wrote it down on the list. Then we ran over to square 17 to see the yellow powder."

"I'll check the ground between here and there, just in case," Stephanie said. "How big is the rabbit?"

"About the size of a peach pit," Kate answered.

"It has lines carved into it for the ears and the legs, and it's light gray," I added.

"Do you think somebody could have taken it out of the tray?" Patti asked when she'd heard the story.

"Who? Everybody was watching the action at square 17," I replied glumly.

Walter Williams was trudging back to square 10, a streak of yellow powder on the knee of his jeans. "Walter, you didn't notice anyone hanging around our square, did you?" I asked him.

He shook his head. "Uh-uh."

Then Stephanie came back, empty-handed. "All I found was a green plastic hair-clip."

"We have to report this to Ms. Anderson," Kate said.

Ms. Anderson wrote down a description of the stone rabbit and asked us to show her exactly where the tray had been sitting when I'd placed the rabbit in it.

"The tray could have gotten jostled in the stampede to square 17," Ms. Anderson pointed out. "The rabbit might have dropped off the tray, fallen back into this hole, or even been kicked into another one. I'll look for it first thing tomorrow morning, as soon as the light is better."

"Green, Hunter, the rest of you — the chariot is waiting," Mr. Civello called from the top of the sloping lawn.

On the ride back, Kyle and Pete Stone were doing imitations of Manthor and Godzilla from the movie, *Godzilla Destroys Manthor*. Jeremy Hendricks, the boy in the red-flannel shirt, ended up on our bus, too. "I'm hitching a ride to Riverhurst to visit my aunt and uncle," he explained.

Jeremy had noticed Roger's cap, and he was

53

telling me that his older brother is the catcher for the Hampton High baseball team. "They've probably even played each other," Jeremy was saying.

I barely heard a word of it, because I was going over the disappearance of the rabbit, again and again, in my mind. I hit the rock with my trowel. Kate and I dug it out. We looked at it. I wrote it down on the list. Then Stephanie yelled about the Yellow Paint People. I put the stone rabbit in the tray, next to the glass and the pipestem. Kate and I raced over to square 17, with Walter Williams calling out behind us. . . .

I suddenly realized I didn't feel Walter's eyes boring into me, so I glanced around for him. I spotted his reddish hair and big ears near the front of the bus. He was talking to a fourth-grade girl with a blond ponytail.

"Fickle," I said to myself. "Thank goodness!"

When we pulled in at Riverhurst Elementary, Jenny Carlin just happened to be pedaling her ten-speed up and down the street.

"She couldn't possibly have known that Pete Stone would be on this bus, could she?" Kate asked sarcastically.

"Dressed to the teeth," Stephanie muttered.

54

Let's just say Jenny looked a lot neater than we did. She was wearing a hot-pink jumpsuit and matching sneakers. We were wearing jeans and sweatshirts decorated with dirt from Chesterfield.

"Okay! Let's go!" Mr. Miller clapped his hands as the bus doors swung open.

I'd started down the aisle when Stephanie grabbed my arm. "What's your hurry?" she whispered, nodding meaningfully at Pete, who was a few kids behind us.

Stephanie made me wait until Pete had squeezed past us. Then she shoved me in line right behind him. When Pete and I got off the bus at the same time, Jenny Carlin almost wrecked her bike on a fire hydrant.

"One for our side," said Patti.

Chapter
6

There's an old saying that good things come in threes, so I was hoping bad things did, too. If they did, I'd already had my bad things: (1) the tiny problem with my perm; (2) the very embarrassing phone call from Jenny and Angela; (3) the disappearance of the stone rabbit. It was time for an upswing, right?

My brother, Roger, of all people, helped with the hair problem. When I got home Saturday afternoon, he said, "It looks a lot like Karen Wessel's hair. You know — the lead singer for Just Plain Folks?"

"It does?" Karen Wessel is really attractive.

"Sure, check out their new video. I really mean

it. All you'd have to do is get the bottom part of your hair organized into those little braids."

"Thanks, Roger." I rushed for the stairs.

"Hey! Can I have my baseball cap back now?"

"Sure!" I threw it down to him and spent the next hour fluffing up the top of my hair, and braiding and rebraiding the bottom. I practiced the next day, too, and I must have gotten it right, because when I went to school on Monday, they raved!

"I can't believe how cool you look, Lauren," Stephanie said.

"Those braids were a great idea," Kate added.

"Roger was right," Patti said. "Just like Karen Wessel."

I was such a big hit at school that I almost got conceited about it. Even Mrs. Mead, our teacher, complimented me as we filed into the classroom. "A very flattering new look, Lauren," she said.

At lunchtime, several fourth- and fifth-grade girls asked Stephanie if she'd consider giving them perms, and there were so many boys sitting at our table in the cafeteria that they had to bring over extra chairs.

Jenny and Angela were facing us across the room. I could see Jenny was absolutely boiling, especially when Pete Stone plopped himself down right next to me.

That's why I thought Jenny Carlin had written the note.

I found it when I walked out to the bike rack with Kate and Patti and Stephanie, after school was over that afternoon. There was a white envelope stuck under the big clip on the back of my bike.

"What's that?" Kate asked.

I lifted the clip and looked at the front of the envelope. "*Lauren Hunter*," it said. My name was typed in capital letters.

"It's the same kind of type as the school's computers," Patti pointed out.

"Don't just stand there. Open it!" Stephanie urged.

I tore open the envelope, unfolded the note inside, and read aloud:

Dear Lauren,

I've admired you from afar, and I think you're the nicest and prettiest girl at Riverhurst Elementary, maybe even in the world. I would like very much to get to know you better.

If you're interested, please meet me in front

58

of the Pizza Palace at the mall, on Tuesday at
four P.M.

Your secret admirer

"Wow!" said Patti, truly impressed.

I wasn't impressed. I was furious! "Where is
she?" I growled.

"Who?" exclaimed Kate and Patti and Stephanie
at the same time.

But I'd already spotted Jenny Carlin.

She was standing near the front steps of the
school with Angela Kemp, looking straight at me, of
course — she didn't want to miss a thing!

I stormed right up to Jenny, waving the note.
"Meet at the Pizza Palace? You didn't honestly think
I'd be dumb enough to go for this twice, did you?"
I practically shrieked in her face.

"What are you talking about?" Jenny said.

"As if you didn't know!" I replied. "This letter,
of course!"

Jenny took the note and started to read it. I knew
she was really reading, because when Jenny reads
silently, her thin little lips move up and down.

Jenny read the note through once, then she read
it through again before raising her big green eyes to

mine. "I didn't write this note, Lauren," she said.

"Give me a break!" I said.

"No, really, I didn't," Jenny insisted. "Would I write something as corny as 'afar'? Even as a joke?" She actually sounded honest — as honest as Jenny gets.

Kate and Patti and Stephanie were standing behind me by that time.

"Good point," Kate murmured.

"I never thought I'd be saying this," Stephanie added, "but I actually believe her."

A blue car honked twice. "That's my mother," Jenny Carlin said coolly. "So if you don't mind . . ." She let the note drop from her hand. "Come on, Angela."

As they made their exit, I picked the note up off the ground. "If Jenny Carlin didn't write this," I wondered out loud, "then who did?"

We guessed all the way home on our bikes.

"Pete Stone," Stephanie suggested.

"He did sit with us coming back from Chesterfield," Kate pointed out.

"I'm sure he's probably never heard the word 'afar,' " I replied.

"Tommy Brown? Alan Reese?" said Kate. They're two other fifth-graders.

"Alan Reese likes Tracy Danner again," I said. "And Tommy Brown's more interested in sports than in girls."

"Don't you think the note sounds _older_ than fifth grade?" Patti asked us.

"That's an idea!" exclaimed Stephanie. "Maybe it's from a sixth-grader, or even seventh!"

"This couldn't be one of Donald Foster's jokes, could it?" I asked nervously.

"No way," said Kate. "A phone call maybe, but not a letter — it's too much trouble." She thought for a second. "What about Jeremy Hendricks?"

"Jeremy Hendricks?" I said. "Hampton is fifteen miles away — how would he be able to stick a note on my bike?"

"Remember his aunt and uncle?" said Patti. "I heard Jeremy telling Kyle that his cousin Sam's on the Riverhurst Junior High soccer team. Maybe Jeremy asked his cousin to deliver the note."

The junior high school _is_ just around the corner from our elementary school.

"And when Sam spotted your bike, he decided

to leave it there instead of hanging around and handing it to you," Stephanie suggested.

My bike has a little license plate on it that says "Lauren H," so I supposed it was possible. . . .

"Jeremy was really talking your ear off on the bus," Kate reminded me.

"Mmmm." Jeremy Hendricks does look a little like Kevin DeSpain, if you get him at the right angle.

"We'll just have to wait and see," Patti said, very practically.

Patti, Kate, and Stephanie were coming to the mall, too, of course. They planned to hide just across from the Pizza Palace in Sweet Stuff, a candy store.

Tuesday morning, I put on my newest pair of Why? jeans and my best long sweater. I was extra careful with my hair — I made five separate braids in the back.

All day long, the four of us were watching the clock. When the final bell rang at three, we practically exploded out of the classroom! We pedaled to the mall so fast that we got there with nearly a half hour to spare.

"We could hang out in Just Juniors," Patti said. "I've got store credit for the blouse I returned."

So she and Kate and Stephanie tried on clothes

for a while. I was too nervous, plus I didn't want to mess up my hair.

"Four minutes to four," Kate announced at last, checking her watch.

We dashed out of Just Juniors and down the main aisle of the mall toward the Pizza Palace and Sweet Stuff.

"Hey, isn't that . . ." Stephanie said, stopping suddenly.

"Who?" I said.

"I thought I saw Jenny Carlin," Stephanie answered, staring through the window of a housewares store. "I guess I was wrong."

"Better hurry," Kate warned. "One minute to four."

As we got close, the three of them veered off to the right side of the aisle, while I kept to the left. "Good luck, Lauren!" they called out before they disappeared into Sweet Stuff.

I slowed down. I wanted to stroll casually into the Pizza Palace, not race in like a nerd, but it wasn't hard for me to see that I'd gotten there first. The Pizza Palace is a tiny room with four video games next to the front door, a long counter with stools in the middle, and a big pizza oven in the back. One old guy

63

was sitting at the counter, drinking a Coke and talking to the cook.

I walked back outside and sat down on a bench in the middle of the main aisle.

Maybe it *was* Jeremy Hendricks after all, I began thinking. He'd have to wait till school was out, and then get somebody to drive him here from Hampton, which would take twenty minutes . . . thirty, if there's traffic. . . . Oh, no! Could he have meant some other mall? Calm down, Lauren — there aren't any other malls between here and Hampton, and no other Pizza Palaces, either.

I sat. And sat. I started to get twitchy. I watched the big hand of the clock in the Sweet Stuff sign move to the five . . . to the ten . . . to the fifteen. My stomach began to churn.

What if Stephanie *did* see Jenny Carlin? I asked myself. Has Jenny put one over on me again? If she has, I'll personally pay her back for this one!

"Lauren?" a voice said behind me. "I'm really glad you waited."

I whirled around . . . and shrieked! "*You*? You wrote the note?"

"Of course," said Walter Williams. "Sorry I'm late. My mom ran out of gas."

The words were hardly out of Walter's mouth when who popped up from behind a large planter but Jenny Carlin and Angela Kemp! They were hooting with laughter.

"This is your secret admirer?" Angela howled. "Isn't he a little short for you, Lauren?"

" 'I think you're the nicest and prettiest girl at Riverhurst Elementary,' " said Jenny, giggling helplessly. She'd memorized the note!

Walter's face went beet red.

"Did your mommy help you write that sweet letter?" Jenny said to him in a baby voice.

Walter gave me one last suffering look. Then he spun around so fast he almost tripped over his own feet. Without another word, he dashed down the main aisle of the mall toward an exit.

What could I say to Jenny and Angela that would make this whole situation seem even one bit less humiliating? Nothing! So I stomped off toward the opposite exit, while they collapsed on the bench in hysterics. They couldn't have been happier if they'd planned it themselves.

"Lauren — wait!" Kate, Stephanie, and Patti caught up with me in front of the housewares store.

"What happened?" Patti said. "What was Walter Williams doing there?"

"And Jenny and Angela?" added Kate. "WBRM was turned up so loud in Sweet Stuff that we couldn't hear a thing anybody was saying," she explained.

"Walter Williams wrote that note," I told them.

"Why didn't we think of it earlier?" said Patti. "Because if you really think about it, he's the only boy at Riverhurst Elementary who *would* write 'I've admired you from afar.' "

"Please!" I moaned. "Why me?"

"And Jenny and Angela saw the whole thing." Stephanie was kind of holding on to her stomach.

"Yeah, they were spying on me from behind a planter," I replied, miserable. I knew I would be able to hear those girls laughing just as clearly when I'm eighty years old! "Could we get out of here?"

"Slowly, okay?" Stephanie started walking sort of bent over.

"What's wrong with you?" I asked her.

"We were in Sweet Stuff too long," she said crossly, hugging her sides. "I had to do something to pass the time."

"Half a pound of chocolate-dipped strawberries and a Rocky Road," said Kate. "To be exact."

66

"Maybe we should stop by Feathers and Fins on the way out," I muttered.

"What for?" Kate asked.

"I thought I'd eat some worms," I said glumly.

"It's not that bad," Patti assured me. "There's no reason for anyone else to even know about this."

But I had a feeling that wasn't what Jenny Carlin was thinking.

Chapter
7

I was right. Jenny Carlin was really busy Wednesday. When Kate, Patti, Stephanie, and I walked into Mrs. Mead's room that morning, Jenny and Angela were huddled in a corner with Erin Wilson and Robin Becker. As soon as Jenny spotted me, she whispered something and smirked, then the four of them sat down.

Right after the bell rang for class to start, I saw Jenny slip a note to Nancy Hersh, who read it and passed it to Sally Mason. By lunchtime, all the girls in 5B knew about Walter.

By the time the final bell rang that afternoon, the whole fifth grade had probably heard the story.

As we unlocked our bikes, I felt as though half the school was snickering at me.

Just when I thought things couldn't get any worse, someone tapped me on the shoulder. "Lauren," Walter Williams said, "I just needed to tell you."

"Give me a break, Walter!" I hissed. I swung onto my bike and was halfway up the block before he could finish.

I wasn't so far away that I couldn't hear some of the guys shout, "Way to go, Walt!"

Even after that, Walter wouldn't leave me alone! Thursday before school, Walter was lurking near the front steps of Riverhurst Elementary. I practically had to knock him down to get past him. That afternoon, he tried to waylay me by the bike rack again, but Kate and Stephanie wheeled my bike around to the back of the building for me, while Patti held him off until I made my getaway.

I'd barely gotten home safely when the telephone rang. For the first time in my life, I made my mom answer it. As soon as she told me it was Walter, I went into the bathroom until I heard her hang up.

I got lucky on Friday — the fourth-graders took a class trip into the city to go to the museum. Lucky until that night, at least. The sleepover was at Stephanie's house.

"I've made up my mind," I announced to Kate, Stephanie, and Patti over one of Mrs. Green's chocolate-chip cookies — we'd brought the whole three dozen, along with Cherry Cokes and Cheetos, into Stephanie's bedroom. "I'm going to stop this craziness with Walter Williams, once and for all, on the bus to Chesterfield tomorrow."

"What are you going to say?" Kate asked me. She was sitting on one of the twin beds, stroking Cinders.

"That he's completely wrecked my reputation at Riverhurst Elementary, and embarrassed me more than I've ever been embarrassed in my life, and if he doesn't leave me alone, I'll . . . I'll . . ."

"You'll what?" said Stephanie.

"I'll . . . talk to his mother!" I said.

"Tattle?" said Kate.

"What choice do I have?" I said.

"I sort of feel sorry for Walter," said Patti.

"But the kid won't take a hint," Kate said. "I don't think Lauren has a choice."

"*Is* that the most embarrassing thing that ever happened to you?" Stephanie asked me.

"Having an eight-year-old meet me for a date, with my worst enemy as a witness?" I said. "I can't think of anything more embarrassing!"

"What about you, Kate?" Stephanie said. "What's the worst thing that you can remember happening to you?"

"Are you crazy?" said Kate. "I'm not telling." She sat down on the floor and grabbed a handful of Cheetos off the tray.

"What's the worst?" Stephanie insisted. "Truth or dare!"

"Truth or dare." Kate thought about it for a minute. She didn't really want to tell the truth. On the other hand, Stephanie's dares could be gruesome, like the time she made Kate phone Robert Ellwanger, the biggest geek in our class, and ask him to go to the movies.

"Oh, all right!" Kate grumbled at last. "Truth. When I was in the first grade, Henry Larkin shoved me off the seesaw, and I wet my pants!"

"Oh, no!" Stephanie giggled. "Did anyone see?"

"Just about everybody at recess," Kate said. "I had to go home and change clothes. It was awful."

"I didn't know that, Kate!" I exclaimed.

"You had the measles that week," Kate said. "I made a plan to run away from home and sail to the South Seas so I'd never have to face anybody again."

"You got over it, though," Patti pointed out. "Lauren, so will you. And Henry Larkin turned out fine." Henry's in 5B and he's really gotten cute. "Maybe there's hope for Walter Williams when he's older."

"If Walter doesn't leave me alone, he'll never get any older," I said darkly.

"Lauren — truth or dare?" Kate said.

"Dare," I replied. "Nothing you think of can equal what I've already been through this week."

Kate grinned at me. "I'll do my best. Run up and touch Tod Schwartz's house."

"Kate!" I groaned. "What if he's home? He'll see me!"

"Tod and Mary Beth always have a date on Friday. It's only ten o'clock — he won't be back, yet," Stephanie pointed out, "unless they're fighting."

"Great!" I muttered. "And what about your parents? They're sitting in the living room — how will I get out of the house?"

"Climb through Stephanie's window," Kate suggested.

"I'll let you out." Stephanie unlatched the screen and started pushing the window up.

I guess Cinders was only pretending to be asleep on Stephanie's pillow. As soon as the window was open about three inches, he shot through the crack like a rocket!

"Cinders!" Stephanie squealed, pushing her window all the way up. "You come back here, bad cat!" She crawled out the window into the side yard with no shoes on. Kate and Patti and I were right behind her. The moon was shining, and there was some light from a street lamp, but I couldn't see the kitten anywhere.

"Where did he go?" Kate whispered.

"If only he weren't so dark," Patti murmured.

Patti's kitten, Adelaide, and my kitten, Rocky, are black, too, but they have white spots. Since Cinders is solid black, he completely disappeared in the shadows.

"There he is!" Stephanie hissed. "He's on the top rail of the fence again, heading for the backyard!"

"Cinders!" we whispered loudly, racing after him.

The kitten could run faster on the fence rail than we could on the ground, where we tripped over

73

bushes and roots and lawn furniture. He'd slow down just enough for us to almost catch him, then race ahead again. He was really enjoying himself.

"This isn't working," Stephanie muttered. She stopped running. "Cinders . . . " she crooned. "I have your mousie. . . ."

Cinders looked over his shoulder.

"Cinders . . ." Stephanie called softly again.

Suddenly an ear-splitting howl practically made my hair go straight!

"What is *that?*" Kate exclaimed.

"How spooky!" whispered Patti with a shiver.

"The Williamses' dog," Stephanie told them. "It's okay. He can't get over here."

But she spoke too soon. There was a terrific crash as the dog threw itself against the other side of the fence . . . and one of the boards slipped sideways!

"Oh, no!" groaned Stephanie, trying to block the hole in the fence with her body.

She wasn't fast enough. A long, spotted dog oozed right through the hole. Cinders took one look and dived off the top fence rail. The kitten dashed toward the Greens' front yard, with the spotted streak in hot pursuit!

"Just wonderful!" Stephanie huffed as we tore after them. "My parents are going to love this!"

"I never thought these words would be coming out of *my* mouth, but where is Walter Williams when we need him?" I yelled over the barking.

Cinders scurried up the little maple tree the Greens had planted next to their front walk and clung to the top branch, spitting and yowling. The long, low dog raced around and around the trunk, yapping its spotted head off.

"Bob, cut that out!" Stephanie ordered.

"Bob?" I asked.

"Yeah, he's named for some relative of Walter's," said Stephanie. "Bob!"

"What is going on out here?" a man thundered.

"Your dad," Patti reported to Stephanie.

"Cinders is stuck up in the tree, Daddy," Stephanie said as Mr. Green hurried down the sidewalk.

"We have one thing to be thankful for," Kate said to me. "At least Donald Foster isn't getting to see this."

Since Donald Foster lives in the house between Kate's and mine, he's gotten an eyeful of all kinds of sleepover messes — and he never lets us forget them.

"Maybe not Donald," Patti murmured. "But isn't that Tod Schwartz's truck just pulling up to the curb?"

Tod and Walter Williams arrived at the maple tree at about the same time. Tod was wearing his red and gold football jacket ("He and Mary Beth must have broken up again," Kate pointed out, "or *she'd* be wearing it."), and he'd gotten his hair cut really short. He looked fabulous, and there we were, barefoot, in our pajamas.

Walter, on the other hand, was wearing his orange down vest and some striped baggies, and his mother was with him. "Mom, this is Lauren," he said.

"Hello, Mrs. Williams. I've — " I began.

"Hello, Lauren," Mrs. Williams interrupted. She was nice-looking, with short brown hair, a pleasant smile, and normal, flat ears. She peered closely at me in the darkness. "You *are* a little like Mindy Lou Hopkins."

"Mindy Lou Hopkins?" I repeated.

I was trying to think if I'd ever seen anyone in the movies or on TV with that name when Mrs. Williams went on, "You remind Walter of his favorite baby-sitter back in Archer City, where we used to live. Of course, Mindy Lou's quite a bit older than you are, but she has the same curly brown hair . . . ."

I'll never get a permanent again!

"Walter has something to say to you," Mrs. Williams told me.

But before anybody could really talk, we had to get Cinders out of the tree. Mrs. Williams grabbed Bob. "He's probably the only half dalmation, half basset in the state," Walter bragged proudly. You know how people sometimes look like their dogs? A basset is exactly what Kate had called Walter!

Mrs. Williams dragged Bob toward the Greens' backyard.

Then Tod said, "We can't lean a ladder against this tree. It'd break, or something. What if I just pick the kid up . . ."

Walter, standing on Tod's big shoulders, managed to pull Cinders out of the maple.

"Poor baby!" said Stephanie, rushing the kitten into the house. Patti and Kate went with her.

Mr. Green walked down to the curb with Tod, and Walter Williams and I sat down on the front steps.

"Listen, Walter," I began. "This business has to stop."

"I know," Walter agreed quickly. "That's one of the things I wanted to tell you. I met a neat girl from 4B on the class trip to the museum today. I like her a lot, so it has to be over between us. Sorry, Lauren."

What? Walter Williams was dumping *me?* I couldn't believe what I was hearing!

Before I could say anything, though, Walter went on. "There's something else, Lauren." He reached into the pocket of his orange vest, then held out his hand. "This is for you."

Walter dropped something small and hard into my palm.

"What is it?" We were sitting in the shadow of an azalea bush, so I held my hand up to the porch light. Small, roundish, dark-gray . . . "The stone rabbit!" I shrieked. "Walter Williams, where did you find this?"

"I didn't *find* it, exactly," Walter mumbled. "I . . . uh . . . took it out of your tray."

"You stole the rabbit out of the tray?" I said. "But why?"

"I wanted you to like me," Walter said. "I was

78

going to pretend that I'd found the rabbit for you, so I could look like a hero."

I scrambled to my feet and glared down at him. "Why didn't you tell me sooner?" I was almost shouting.

"I tried to, Lauren. You wouldn't listen to me," Walter answered.

"Thanks a lot!" I turned my back on him and opened the Greens' front door.

"Lauren . . ." Walter said meekly.

"Now what?"

"My parents have grounded me for a month as punishment for taking the rabbit," he told me. "I just wondered . . ."

"Wondered what?" I snapped impatiently.

". . . if maybe you wouldn't have to tell Ms. Anderson the whole story. I'd kind of hate for Linda — that's the girl I met — to hear about it at school." Walter peered up at me through his round glasses.

"I'll think about it." I angrily stepped into the house and slammed the door closed behind me. I was not happy, and my mood didn't improve when I walked into Stephanie's room in time to hear the deejay on WBRM announce, "And now, our latest request is from Walter W. to Lauren H., 'You're My One and Only Love.' "

"Walter didn't do that," I said. "He has a new girlfriend."

"One point for Jenny Carlin," the four of us said at the same time.

Chapter
8

I was furious with Walter Williams Friday night. But on the bus the next morning, he looked so small and defenseless that I didn't have the heart to squeal on him. After all, if *I* don't know how awful it is to have stories going around about you, who does?

"So what are you going to tell Ms. Anderson?" Stephanie asked as we squeezed into the back seat of the bus.

"I'll think of something," I said. "What's important is getting the rabbit back to her, right?"

Ms. Anderson was talking to one of the university students in the parking lot when we got to Chesterfield. She spotted me right away.

"I'm afraid we didn't find your rabbit," she told me.

"That's all right," I said. "It turned up after all. I'm really sorry, Ms. Anderson." I handed her the stone rabbit.

"Why, that's terrific, Lauren! Where on earth did you find it?"

I could feel my face getting hot at the thought of telling Ms. Anderson about Walter. I guess I was blushing, too, because she said, "Well, that's not really important. What's important is that the rabbit is back."

She studied the stone closely. "This is the most unusual — I've never seen a carving like this around here. Maybe it was traded to the Indians of Riverhurst by a tribe from farther south . . . I'll have to do some research."

Then she gave me a big hug. "Thanks, Lauren. A really important find! And we'll just keep this little mix-up to ourselves, okay?"

Walter Williams was lurking around on the gravel path leading up to the house. When I made a thumbs-up sign, his face broke into a huge smile. Walter's really not bad-looking when he smiles — for a fourth-grader, that is.

Kate and Stephanie and Patti and I had a great time that day. First Ms. Anderson showed all the kids what she'd found in square 17, where the graduate students had been digging out the yellow powder.

"It *was* an Indian grave," she told us, folding back a cover of brown oilcloth that kept the hole dry. "These are the bones of an Indian boy about fifteen years old. He was buried facing the river, with arrowheads and fishhooks around him so that he could find food in the next life. It's kind of peaceful, isn't it?"

Ms. Anderson was right. It wasn't at all creepy, even though Kyle Hubbard started humming the theme song from *The Mummy's Tomb*. The Indian boy had been laid on his side, as if he were sleeping. He had a stone bracelet on his left wrist and a necklace of blue beads around his neck.

Even Stephanie didn't say, "Gross!" In fact, she said, "Kind of neat!"

"We're sure there are more graves on the Chesterfield estate," Ms. Anderson said. "So good luck with your work today."

Our group cleaned stuff that morning, like last time. Then we took a break for lunch. My mom had packed a pile of roast beef sandwiches and lots of potato salad, so Kyle Hubbard, Pete Stone, Jeremy Hendricks, and two of his friends, Andrew and Max, ate with us.

Walter came to talk to me that afternoon, while we were digging in our old squares, 8 and 10.

"Thanks, Lauren," he said. "Now I'm going to do something really nice for you."

I shook my head, hard! "Please don't, Walter," I said. "The things you do for me have a way of turning out . . . not quite right."

"This will, though," said Walter. "I've thought it through, I promise."

I forgot all about it, because just about then, two newspaper reporters and a photographer arrived at Chesterfield to do an article for the Riverhurst paper.

First Ms. Anderson showed them the Indian grave. Then she brought them over to square 8.

"This is the girl I was telling you about, Lauren . . ."

"Hunter," I said. "Lauren Hunter."

"She made one of the most important finds of this dig," Ms. Anderson said to the reporters, "a carved stone rabbit that indicates the Indians that lived here may have been part of an extensive trading network."

84

Ms. Anderson said a lot more, and the photographer took a picture of me holding the rabbit. "You'll be in the Monday edition," she told me. "Maybe even the front page."

Stephanie, Kate, and Patti grinned at me. "One for our side," they said.

Jenny Carlin almost died when the Riverhurst Elementary principal, Mrs. Wainwright, stopped into 5B with a copy of the paper on Monday afternoon. She held it up for the whole class to see, and there I was with the stone rabbit, smiling at the camera.

"Good for you, Lauren," said Mrs. Wainwright. "And for all of you who participated in this after-school activity."

I thought nothing could gripe Jenny more than that, but I hadn't counted on Walter Williams.

He waited until school was dismissed and all the kids were milling around outside the building. Kate, Stephanie, Patti, and I were headed for the bike rack. Jenny Carlin and Angela Kemp were standing near the curb, waiting for Jenny's mother's car.

Suddenly I heard a creaky voice screech, "Jenny, the Pizza Palace at four, right? You did say *this afternoon* at *four* o'clock?'' Walter Williams smiled politely.

Jenny's face turned purple. She and Angela were so shocked they couldn't say a word.

"See you then," Walter bellowed. "I'll try not to be late!"

And I thought the kid wasn't a genius?

"Way to go, Walt!" Kyle and Pete and the other guys on the front steps shouted.

As we got on our bikes and rode away, Stephanie licked her index finger and drew a big "1" in the air.

Game-winning point for the Sleepover Friends!

#9 *No More Sleepovers, Patti?*

We carried the trays of snacks down the hall to Stephanie's room. As soon as we closed the door behind us, Kate said to Patti, "You haven't told us — did you talk your parents out of moving to Alaska?"

Patti frowned unhappily. "No — I just *couldn't* say anything. They're so excited about all the advantages for Horace and me. . . ."

"What advantages?" I wanted to know.

"Oh, like incredibly clean air and wide open spaces — " Patti began.

"Let's eat before the food gets cold," Kate said brightly, changing the subject.

But I don't think anyone was hungry. I'm usually starving, and even I had no appetite at all. Were we really losing a Sleepover Friend?

Pack your bags for fun and adventure with

SLEEPOVER FRIENDS™
by Susan Saunders

Join Kate, Lauren, Stephanie and Patti at their great sleepover parties every weekend. Truth or Dare, scary movies, late-night boy talk—it's all part of **Sleepover Friends!**

Get ready for fun!

- ☐ 40641-8 **Patti's Luck #1**
- ☐ 40642-6 **Starring Stephanie #2**
- ☐ 40643-4 **Kate's Surprise #3**
- ☐ 40644-2 **Patti's New Look #4**
- ☐ 41336-8 **Lauren's Big Mix-Up #5**
- ☐ 41337-6 **Kate's Camp-Out #6**
- ☐ 41694-4 **Stephanie Strikes Back #7**

PREFIX CODE 0-590-

Available wherever you buy books… or use the coupon below.
$2.50 each.

Lots of Fun... Tons of Trouble!

by Ann M. Martin

Kristy, Claudia, Mary Anne, Stacey, and Dawn – they're the Baby-sitters Club!

The five girls at Stoneybrook Middle School get into all kinds of adventures...with school, boys, and, of course, baby-sitting!

Join the Club and join the fun!

☐ 33950-8	**Kristy's Great Idea #1**	**$2.50**
☐ 33951-6	**Claudia and the Phantom Phone Calls #2**	**$2.50**
☐ 33952-4	**The Truth About Stacey #3**	**$2.50**
☐ 33953-2	**Mary Anne Saves the Day #4**	**$2.50**
☐ 40747-3	**Dawn and the Impossible Three #5**	**$2.50**
☐ 40748-1	**Kristy's Big Day #6**	**$2.50**
☐ 41041-5	**Claudia and Mean Janine #7**	**$2.50**
☐ 41040-7	**Boy-Crazy Stacey #8**	**$2.50**
☐ 41123-3	**The Ghost at Dawn's House #9**	**$2.75**
☐ 41124-1	**Logan Likes Mary Anne #10**	**$2.75**
☐ 41125-X	**Kristy and the Snobs #11**	**$2.75**
☐ 41126-8	**Claudia and the New Girl #12**	**$2.75**
☐ 41127-6	**Good-bye Stacey, Good-bye #13**	**$2.75**
☐ 41128-4	**Hello, Mallory #14**	**$2.75**
☐ 41588-3	**Baby-sitters on Board! Special Edition**	**$2.95**
☐ 41587-5	**Little Miss Stoneybrook and Dawn #15**	**$2.75**

PREFIX CODE 0-590-

APPLE® PAPERBACKS

More books you'll love, filled with mystery, adventure, friendship, and fun!

NEW APPLE TITLES

☐ 40388-5 **Cassie Bowen Takes Witch Lessons**
Anna Grossnickle Hines $2.50
☐ 33824-2 **Darci and the Dance Contest**   Martha Tolles $2.50
☐ 40494-6 **The Little Gymnast**   Sheila Haigh $2.50
☐ 40403-2 **A Secret Friend**   Marilyn Sachs $2.50
☐ 40402-4 **The Truth About Mary Rose**   Marilyn Sachs $2.50
☐ 40405-9 **Veronica Ganz**   Marilyn Sachs $2.50

BEST-SELLING APPLE TITLES

☐ 33662-2 **Dede Takes Charge!**   Johanna Hurwitz $2.50
☐ 41042-3 **The Dollhouse Murders**   Betty Ren Wright $2.50
☐ 40755-4 **Ghosts Beneath Our Feet**   Betty Ren Wright $2.50
☐ 40950-6 **The Girl With the Silver Eyes**   Willo Davis Roberts $2.50
☐ 40605-1 **Help! I'm a Prisoner in the Library**   Eth Clifford $2.50
☐ 40724-4 **Katie's Baby-sitting Job**   Martha Tolles $2.50
☐ 40725-2 **Nothing's Fair in Fifth Grade**   Barthe DeClements $2.50
☐ 40382-6 **Oh Honestly, Angela!**   Nancy K. Robinson $2.50
☐ 33894-3 **The Secret of NIMH**   Robert C. O'Brien $2.25
☐ 40180-7 **Sixth Grade Can Really Kill You**   Barthe DeClements $2.50
☐ 40874-7 **Stage Fright**   Ann M. Martin $2.50
☐ 40305-2 **Veronica the Show-off**   Nancy K. Robinson $2.50
☐ 41224-8 **Who's Reading Darci's Diary?**   Martha Tolles $2.50
☐ 41119-5 **Yours Till Niagara Falls, Abby**   Jane O'Connor $2.50

Available wherever you buy books...or use the coupon below.

Scholastic Inc. P.O. Box 7502, 2932 E. McCarty Street, Jefferson City, MO 65102

Please send me the books I have checked above. I am enclosing $_____
(please add $1.00 to cover shipping and handling). Send check or money order-no cash or C.O.D.'s please.

Name_____

Address_____

City_____ State/Zip_____

Please allow four to six weeks for delivery. Offer good in U.S.A. only. Sorry, mail order not available to residents of Canada.
Prices subject to change.   APP987